The Ugly Duckling

Hans Christian Andersen

It was very pleasant out in the country. It was summer time, the corn was yellow, the oats green, the hay was stacked down in the green meadows, and there the stork walked about on his long red legs and talked Egyptian. He had learnt the language from his mother. Round the fields and meadows there were large woods and within them deep lakes: indeed, it was pleasant out in the country. Full in the sunshine, an old manor house stood, surrounded by a deep moat, and from the base of the walls right down to the water great dock plants grew--so tall that a little child could stand upright under the largest of them. It was as lonely in among them as in the thickest wood; and there a Duck was sitting on her nest. She had got to hatch out her little Ducklings, but by this time she was well nigh tired out, they took so long about it, and she had very few callers. The other Ducks preferred out far beyond the other side of the garden, right into the parson's field--but I've never been there. You're all there, I suppose?" and she got up. "No, that's not all; there lies the biggest egg still. How long will it take? I'm really almost sick of it," and with that she sat down again.

"Well, how goes it?" asked an elderly Duck who came to call on her. "Oh, this one egg takes a dreadful long time," said the sitting Duck; "it won't break. But just you look at the others! They are the sweetest Ducklings I've ever seen; they're all just like their wretch of a father, who never comes to see me."

"Let me look at the egg that won't hatch," said the old Duck; "you may be sure that's a turkey's egg. I was made a fool of once that way, and I had my share of trouble and anxiety with the young ones, I can tell you, for they are afraid of the water. I couldn't get them to go in! I quacked and I pecked, but it was no good. Let me see the egg. Ah, yes, that's a turkey's egg; you just let it lie and teach the rest to swim."

"Oh, I'll just sit on it a bit longer," said the Duck. "As I've sat so long, I may as well give it a Whitsun week!" [1] "Just as you please," said the old Duck, and walked off.

At last the big egg opened. "Pip! pip!" said the young one, scrambling out; he was very big and ugly. The Duck looked at him: "That's a fearfully big Duckling, that is," she said. "None of the others look like that. I suppose it can't be a turkey poult! Well, we'll soon see; into the water he shall go, if I have to kick him out myself."

Next day the weather was perfectly delicious: the sun shone all over the green docks, and the mother Duck and all her family came out, and down to the moat. Splash! Into the water went she. "Quack, quack!" she said, and one Duckling after another plumped in. The water went over their heads, but they were up again in a moment and swam beautifully. Their legs worked of themselves, and now they were all out in the water, and even the ugly grey one was swimming with them. "No, no, that's no turkey," she said. "Look how nicely he uses his legs, and how well he holds himself up. That's my own child! He's really quite handsome if you look at him properly. Quack, quack! Come along with me and I'll take you out into the world and introduce you to the duck-yard, but mind and keep close to me so that nobody can tread on you, and do look out for the cat."

So they went into the duck-yard. There was a terrible commotion there, for two families were quarrelling over an eel's head--which the cat got after all.

"Look, that's the way the world goes," said the mother Duck--her beak watering a little, for she would have liked the eel's head herself. "Now then, use your legs," she said; "mind and look alive, and stoop your necks to the old Duck over there, she's the most distinguished person here; she's of Spanish descent, so she's something special, and you see she's got a red rag round her leg. That is an extraordinarily splendid thing, the greatest distinction any duck can have; it means that people can't do without her, and she must be recognized by animals and men alike. Now then, look alive! Don't turn your toes in! A duckling that's properly brought up keeps its legs wide apart, like father and mother. Look here! Now then! Make a bow and say quack."

So they did; but the other ducks round them looked at them and said, quite loud, "Look there! Now we've got to have all this mob on the top of us, as if there weren't enough of us already; and poof! what an object that duckling is! We can't stand him"; and a duck rushed at him and bit him in the neck.

"Let him be," said his mother; "he isn't doing any harm." "Yes, but he's too big and odd altogether," said the duck who had bitten him; "so he's got to be smacked."

"Those are pretty ducklings that mother has," said the old Duck with the rag on her leg; "all quite pretty except that one. He hasn't been a success; I could wish the mother would alter him."

"That can't be done, your grace," said the mother Duck. "He's not handsome, but he has a really good disposition, and swims as nicely as any of the rest, even better, I venture to say. I believe he will grow handsome, or perhaps in time he will grow even somewhat smaller; he has lain too long in the egg, and so has not acquired a proper shape." And she picked at his neck and smoothed him down. "Besides, he's a drake," she went on, "so it doesn't matter quite so much. He has, I believe, a good constitution and will win through in the end."

"The other ducklings are charming," said the old lady. "Well, make yourselves at home, and if you happen to find an eel's head, you can bring it to me."

So they made themselves at home: but the poor Duckling who had come last out of the egg and looked so ugly, was bitten and buffeted and made to look a fool by the hens and the ducks alike. "He's too big," they all said; and the turkey cock, who was born with spurs, and considered himself an emperor on the strength of it, blew himself up like a ship under full sail and went straight at the Duckling, gobbling and getting quite red in the head. The poor Duckling didn't know where to stay or which way to go, he was so miserable at being ugly and the butt of the whole duck-yard.

That was the first day, and as time went on it got worse and worse. The wretched Duckling was chased about by everybody, and even his mother and sisters were nasty to him, and kept saying: "I wish the cat would get you, you ugly devil." And his mother said: "I wish you'd get right away"; and the ducks bit him and the hens pecked him, and the maid who had to feed the creatures kicked at him. So he ran away, and flew over the fence. The little birds in the bushes shot up in the air in a fright. "That's because I'm so ugly," the Duckling thought, and shut his eyes, but ran on all the same, till he got out into the wide marsh where the wild-duck lived; and there he lay all night, for he was very tired and very unhappy.

In the morning the wild-duck flew up and caught sight of their new comrade. "What sort of a chap are you?" they asked; and the Duckling turned to this side and that and greeted them as well as he could. "You're precious ugly," said the wild-ducks; "but that doesn't matter to us as long as you don't marry into our family." Poor wretch! He wasn't thinking much about marrying, as long as he could be allowed to lie among the reeds, and drink a little marsh water. There he lay two whole days, and then came a pair of wild geese (or rather wild ganders, for they were both he's): they hadn't been hatched out very long, and so they were particularly lively. "Here, mate," they said, "you're so ugly I quite like you. Will you come along and be a migrant? Close by in another marsh there's some sweet pretty wild geese--all young ladies that can say Quack. You're so ugly you could make your fortune with them." At that moment there was a Bang! Bang! and both the wild geese fell dead among the reeds, and the water was stained blood red. Another bang! bang! and whole flights of geese flew up from the reeds, and there was yet another bang! a great shoot was afoot. The sportsmen were all round the marsh, some even sitting up among the branches of trees that stretched out over the reeds. The blue smoke drifted like clouds, in among the dark stems, and hung far out over the water. The dogs went splash! splash! into the mud, and the reeds and rushes swayed hither and thither; it was terrible for the wretched Duckling, who was bending his neck to get it under his wing, when all at once, close to him, there was a fearful big dog with his tongue hanging right out of his mouth and his eyes shining horribly. He thrust his muzzle right at the Duckling and showed his sharp teeth--and then-- splash! Off he went without seizing him.

"Oh, thank goodness," sighed the Duckling; "I'm so ugly, even the dog doesn't like to bite me!" But there he lay perfectly still while the duck shots rattled in the reeds and gun after gun banged out. It was well on in the day before all was quiet,

but the unhappy bird dared
not get up even then. He
waited several hours yet,
before he looked about him,
and then he hurried away
from the marsh as fast as
ever he could, running over
fields and meadows, and
such a wind got up that he
had hard work to get along.
Towards evening he was
near a poor little cottage, so
crazy was it that it didn't
know which way to tumble
down, so it remained
standing. The wind howled
so fiercely round the
Duckling that he had to sit
down on his tail to keep
facing it, and it grew worse
and worse. Then he noticed
that one hinge of the door
was gone, and it hung so
crooked that he could slip
indoors through the crack,
and so he did.

Here lived an old woman
with a cat and a hen. The
cat, whom she called Sonny,
could set up his fur and purr,
and also throw out sparks,
but for this he had to be

stroked backwards. The Hen had very short little legs, and was consequently called "chicky short legs". She laid good eggs, and the woman was as fond of her as of a child of her own.

Next morning the strange Duckling was noticed at once, and the cat began to purr, and the Hen to cluck. "What's the matter?" said the old woman, looking all about her. But her sight wasn't good, so she took the Duckling for a fat duck that had strayed away. "That's a splendid catch," she said: "now I can have duck eggs, if only it isn't a drake! We must make sure of that." So the Duckling was taken in on approval for three weeks, but no eggs came.

The Cat was the gentleman of the house and the Hen the lady, and they always talked of "we and the world"; for they considered that they were half the world, and much the best half. It seemed to the Duckling that some people might think differently, but this the Hen could not tolerate.

"Can you lay eggs?" she asked. "No! Then will you kindly hold your tongue."

And the Cat said: "Can you put up your fur, or purr, or give out sparks? No! Then you've no call to have an opinion when sensible people are talking."

So the Duckling lay in a corner and was in the lowest spirits. He began to think of the fresh air and sunshine, and such a strange longing to swim in the water came on him that he could not help telling the Hen.

"What's the matter with you?" she asked. "You've nothing to do, that's why you get these fancies; you just lay some eggs, or purr, and they'll pass off." "But it is so delicious to float on the water," said the Duckling; "so lovely to get it over your head and dive right down to the bottom."

"Oh yes, most delightful, of course!" said the Hen. "Why, you're absolutely mad! Ask the Cat--he's the cleverest man I know--whether he enjoys floating on the water or diving down; I say nothing of myself. Why, ask your mistress, the old woman; there's no one in the world cleverer than her--do you suppose she wants to go swimming and getting the water over her head?"

"You don't understand me," said the Duckling.

"Well, if we don't understand you, who is going to understand you, pray? You'll never be cleverer than the Cat and the woman, to say nothing of me. Don't give yourself airs, child, but thank your Maker for all the kindness people have done you. Don't you live in a warm room among company you can learn something from? But there! You're a rubbishy thing, and there's little entertainment in your company. You may take it from me! I mean well by you, and I'm telling you home truths, and that's how people can see their true friends. Now just do take pains to lay eggs, or learn to purr or else give sparks."

"I think I'll go out into the wide world," said the Duckling.

"Very well, do," said the Hen.

So the Duckling went off and swam on the water and dived into it; but he was looked down upon by all the creatures because of his ugliness.

Autumn now came on: the leaves of the wood turned brown and yellow, the wind caught them and made them dance about, and above the sky looked cold, where the clouds hung heavy with hail and snow, and on the fence the raven perched and cried "Caw! Caw!" for the mere cold. Indeed, it regularly gave you the shivers to think of it. The unhappy Duckling had a very hard time.

One evening, when there was a lovely sunset, a whole flock of beautiful great birds rose out of the bushes. The Duckling had never seen any so handsome. They were brilliantly white, with long supple necks. They were swans, and they uttered a strange sound and spread their splendid long wings and flew far away from the cold region to warmer lands, and unfrozen lakes. They mounted so high, so high that the ugly little Duckling was strangely moved; he whirled himself round in the water like a wheel, he stretched his neck straight up into the air after them and uttered such a loud cry, so strange, that he was quite frightened at it himself. Oh, he could not forget those beautiful birds, those wonderful birds! And the moment they were out of sight he dived right down to the bottom of the water, and when he came up again he was almost beside himself. He didn't know what the birds were called or which way they were flying, but he loved them as he had never loved anything yet. He was not envious of them--how could it enter his mind to wish for such beauty for himself--he would have been happy if even the ducks had let him into their company--poor ugly creature.

The winter grew very very cold: the Duckling was obliged to swim about on the water to keep it from freezing quite over, but every night the hole he swam in became smaller and smaller. It froze so hard that the ice cracked again; the Duckling had always to be moving about to keep the water open, till at last he was tired out and sat still, and was frozen fast in the ice.

Early in the morning a labourer came that way, saw him, went on the ice and with his wooden shoe broke it up and carried the Duckling home to his wife, and there he was brought to life again. The children wanted to play with him, but he thought they meant to hurt him, and in his fright he dashed right into the milk-pan and made the milk splash out into the room. The woman screamed and

threw up her hands. Then
he flew into the butter-tub
and after that into the meal-
bin and out again.
Goodness, what a sight he
was! The woman screamed
out and hit at him with the
tongs, and the children
tumbled over one another
trying to catch him,
laughing, calling out--by
good luck the door stood
open, and out he rushed
into the bushes, on the new
fallen snow, and there he lay
almost in a swoon.

But it would be too sad to
tell of all the hardships and
miseries which he had to go
through in that hard winter.
When the sun began once
more to shine out warm and
the larks to sing, he was
lying among the reeds in the
marsh, and it was the
beautiful spring. Then all at
once he lifted his wings, and
they rustled more strongly
than before, and bore him
swiftly away; and before he
knew it he was in a spacious
garden where were apple

trees in blossom, and sweet-smelling lilacs hung on long green boughs right down to the winding moat. Oh, it was lovely here, and fresh with spring; and straight in front of him, out of the shadows, came three beautiful white swans with rustling plumage floating lightly on the water. The Duckling recognized the splendid creatures, and a strange sorrowfulness came over him.

"I will fly to them, these royal birds, and they will peck me to death because I, who am so ugly, dare to approach them; but it doesn't matter; it's better to be killed by them than to be snapped at by the ducks and pecked at by hens and kicked by the servant who looks after the poultry-yard, and suffer all the winter." So he flew out into the open water and swam towards the stately swans, and they saw him and hastened with swelling plumage to meet him. "Yes, kill me," the poor creature said, bowing his head down to the water, and waited for death. But what did he see in the clear water? He beheld his own image, but it was no longer that of a clumsy dark grey bird, ugly and repulsive. He was a swan himself.

It doesn't matter in the least
whether you are born in the
duck-yard, if only you've lain
in a swan's egg.

It really delighted him now
to think of all the hardships
and adversities he had
suffered, now he could
rightly discern his good
fortune and all the beauty
that greeted him. The great
swans swam round him and
caressed him with their bills.
Some little children now
came into the garden and
threw bread and corn into
the water, and the smallest
of them cried: "There's a
new one!" And the others
called out in delight: "Yes,
there's a new one come!"
They clapped their hands
and danced about and ran

to their father and mother. More bread and cake was thrown into the water, and everyone said: "The new one is the handsomest of all; how young and beautiful he is!" And the elder swans bowed before him.

At that he felt quite ill at ease, and covered his head with his wings, and knew not what to do. He was more than happy, and yet not proud, for a good heart is never puffed up. He thought how persecuted and depressed he had been, yet now he heard everyone saying he was the most beautiful of all beautiful birds. And the lilacs bowed their branches down to the water, and the sun shone warm and pleasant, and his plumage ruffled, and he raised his slender neck, and from his heart he said joyfully: "Such happiness I never dreamed of when I was the Ugly Duckling."

FOOTNOTE:

[1] This needs a note, for the gist of which I have to thank kind friends in Denmark. 'Whitsun week' is meant to render 'Dyrehavstid', which should be 'Dyrehavsbakketid'. Dyrehavsbakken is a place of amusement near Klampenborg, which used to have a 'season' from Midsummer Day (June 24), to the feast of the Visitation (July 2).

Made in United States
North Haven, CT
29 April 2022